Ghostville Elementary®

Frights!
Camera! Action!

Find out more spooky secrets about

Ghostville Elementary®

Ghostville Elementary®

Frights! Camera! Action!

by Marcia Thornton Jones
and
Debbie Dadey

illustrated by Guy Francis

A
LITTLE APPLE
PAPERBACK

SCHOLASTIC INC.
New York   Toronto   London   Auckland   Sydney
Mexico City   New Delhi   Hong Kong   Buenos Aires

No part of this publication may be reproduced, stored in a retrieval system, or transmitted in any form or by any means, electronic, mechanical, photocopying, recording, or otherwise, without written permission of the publisher. For information regarding permission, write to Scholastic Inc., Attention: Permissions Department, 557 Broadway, New York, NY 10012.

ISBN 0-439-67811-0

12 11 10 9 8 7 6 5 4 3 2   5 6 7 8 9 10/0

Printed in the U.S.A.   40
First printing, November 2005

For Steve...for being so patient while I "interviewed" the ghosts at French Lick!
—MTJ

For Alex Dadey and all his buddies at Werner Elementary
—DD

Contents

THE LEGEND
*Sleepy Hollow Elementary School's
Online Newspaper*

**This Just In: Ghostville Elementary
will be in the movies!**

Breaking News: Can you believe a movie is going to be filmed right here at Sleepy Hollow Elementary? If that wasn't exciting enough, some kids might even get to be extras! Tryouts are at the end of this week.

Why did the moviemakers choose our school? Somehow they heard that everyone calls the school Ghostville Elementary. They also need a cheap, creepy site for filming and our basement is just the place. Who knows? Maybe a *real* ghost will show up to make the movie truly exciting!

Stay tuned for more breaking news.

Your friendly fifth-grade reporter,
Justin Thyme

1
Big News

"Why do we have to do this?" Jeff complained as he cut another article out of the newspaper and pasted it onto a hand-made chart.

Cassidy shrugged and glanced at their teacher. Mr. Morton was in front of the class helping two other third graders with their current-events chart. "I guess Mr. Morton wants us to learn about what's happening in the world," Cassidy said.

Their friend Nina sat cross-legged on the floor beside them and turned the pages of a newspaper. Her long black hair fell onto the paper. She held up a picture of an ice-skater. "Look, here's Michelle Kwan. I wish I could skate like she does."

Cassidy pointed to a blank area of their

chart. "Cut out that picture," she said. "You can put Michelle in the sports section."

Nina shivered and reached for the scissors. She knew what was making her cold, and it wasn't the picture of ice. A ghost was nearby. Nina, Cassidy, and Jeff had learned to recognize the chilly sensation they felt when a ghost was about to show up.

Sure enough, green sparkles appeared

2

near the three kids. Jeff quickly looked around the room as the green sparkles turned into a young girl and a brown dog. No one else in the classroom paid any attention to the ghosts. For some reason, only Jeff, Nina, and Cassidy could see them. The school ghosts chose who they appeared to. The three kids had found out that their basement room was haunted by not one, but an entire class of ghost kids — and ghost pets, too!

The ghost dog, Huxley, sniffed at the newspapers, but the young ghost girl stared at the article Nina held in her hand. "Hi, Becky," Nina whispered to the ghost.

"Let me see that," Becky said, reaching out a glowing green hand. Becky touched the picture, but her hand went all the way through the paper. Becky scrunched up her face and concentrated hard. Then she grabbed the picture.

Jeff glanced around the room again to make sure no one saw the newspaper article floating in the air.

"She's like a dancer," Becky said softly. "I *adore* her flowing skirt."

"She's famous," Cassidy told her.

Becky nodded and the article dropped to the ground. "Famous. That sounds so wonderful!"

Becky twirled away. She floated above the teacher in her own private dance. Mr. Morton continued helping a girl named Barbara with her chart. He didn't know that a ghost spun in circles above his head.

"Watch it," Jeff snapped. But it was too late. Huxley's wagging tail knocked over a bottle of glue. Glue and scraps of newspaper stuck to Huxley's tail. For some reason, Huxley didn't have to concentrate hard to touch unghostly things, even though the other ghosts did. It was as natural to him as wagging his tail.

Cassidy snatched the paper off Huxley's tail before anyone in the class-room could see it waving around in midair. Jeff saved the glue from spilling all over the floor and tried to pet Huxley on the head. His hand went right through the dog's forehead. Jeff liked Huxley, but he would have preferred a real dog.

Nina smoothed out the crumpled news-paper. "Wow!" she exclaimed. "You guys are never going to believe this. Here's an article calling for extras on a movie set. A famous director named Steven Bloodsaw is coming to Sleepy Hollow to make a movie."

"This is my chance!" Jeff shouted, for-getting about Huxley and the chart project. "I'm finally going to be famous!"

The kids were so excited about the movie that they didn't notice that Becky had stopped spinning. She floated above them, listening very carefully and smiling.

2
Chiller

"What's going on?" a kid named Andrew asked, pushing his way past his classmates to reach Jeff.

A whole group of kids crowded around Jeff to find out what he was yelling about. Mr. Morton clapped his hands. "Students, please get back to work."

A girl named Darla interrupted. "What did you find . . ."

". . . in the newspaper?" her twin sister, Carla, finished.

Carla and Darla not only looked alike and sounded alike, but they also had a habit of finishing each other's sentences.

Nina smiled. "A movie is being shot right here in Sleepy Hollow by a famous director. They're hiring local people to be extras in the movie. It's called *Chillers*."

Jeff puffed out his chest. He was proud to share his knowledge of moviemaking. "Extras are the people who are in the crowd or background scenes during a movie."

Cassidy hurried to one of the classroom computers while the rest of the class leaned over Jeff to read the newspaper article. Even Mr. Morton cleaned his glasses and read the paper. Everyone had forgotten about the chart project.

Cassidy loved looking up things on the Internet for more information. Green glitter sparkled above the computer, and Cassidy found she wasn't the only one interested. Two ghosts floated so close to the screen that Cassidy had to wave them away. Becky and her older brother, Ozzy, hovered above Cassidy's shoulder to see what she was doing. Ozzy usually liked to make trouble, but today he was quiet and very curious.

"Here it is," Cassidy said when she found the site for *Chiller*. She read out loud from the computer screen, "The movie is a ghost story set during the time period that the original Sleepy Hollow Elementary existed."

Andrew pushed past Jeff and leaned over Cassidy's shoulder. He didn't even notice the cold chill as Ozzy was forced out of the way. "That director will want to use my house," Andrew bragged. Andrew was very proud of the fact that his parents had recently bought the oldest and

biggest house in Sleepy Hollow, the historic Blackburn Estate.

"It says that the director is looking for 'local talent' to appear in the movie," Cassidy told the class. "A casting call for extras has been made for tomorrow. Right here in our school!"

Jeff wiggled his way past Nina, Carla, and Darla until he stood right beside the computer. It was no secret that Jeff loved movies and acting. "I'm going to be the star of *Chiller*," Jeff bragged. "Just you wait and see!"

3
Wilma Fudgebottom

"This is the biggest thing to ever happen in Sleepy Hollow," Jeff said. He linked arms with Nina and Cassidy to hurry them down the sidewalk.

It was early Saturday morning. Very early. Nina hopped over a crack in the sidewalk. "It's barely light out," she said through a yawn. "Couldn't this wait until later?"

Jeff shook his head and walked even faster. "I want to be first to audition for the starring role," he said for at least the thirteenth time.

Cassidy pulled her arm loose from Jeff's grip. "If this Steven Bloodsaw is such a hotshot moviemaker, then why is he holding auditions at our dinky little elementary school?" she asked.

"Sleepy Hollow Elementary is the perfect setting," Jeff told her. "It has a stage, and the school dates back to when the ghost story takes place. He's even planning on shooting some of the scenes right there in the basement."

"Our basement has its very own ghosts," Nina pointed out.

"Nobody knows that except us," Cassidy said.

Their school was nicknamed Ghostville Elementary because — for as long as even their parents could remember — there had been stories that Sleepy Hollow Elementary was haunted. To everyone else, they were just that. Stories. Only Nina, Cassidy, and Jeff knew the stories

were true. They also knew the ghosts only haunted the basement.

The kids hurried toward their school and pulled open the door. "Oh, no," Jeff groaned.

"It looks like you're not the only one who set an alarm clock," Cassidy said. A long line of people snaked down the hall and around the corner. Moms, dads,

grandparents, and kids from their class stood waiting. It looked liked everybody in town wanted a part in the movie.

"Excuse me. Excuse me," Jeff mumbled as he pushed his way through the crowd.

"Hey," a man wearing a suit said. "The line starts back there."

"You don't understand," Jeff said. "I have to get to the front of the line."

"Forget it, kid," said a woman wearing a long sparkly dress and high heels.

Andrew stuck out his thumb. "Move your carcass all the way to the back," he told Jeff.

Carla nodded. "After all . . ."

". . . we were here first," Darla finished.

"This stinks," Jeff said as Cassidy and Nina pulled him back to the end of the line behind Carla and Darla.

"But it is fair," Nina pointed out.

"I could save Mr. Bloodsaw a lot of time," Jeff told her. "Once the director sees my audition, he can send the rest of these people home."

Jeff muttered and mumbled as the line inched forward. The second hand on the hallway clock slowly crept around.

"This is ridiculous," Jeff said when they turned the corner and were almost to the door of the gymnasium, where the auditions were being held. "I'm tired of wasting everyone's time." Before Nina or Cassidy could stop him, Jeff waved to one of the members of the movie crew standing by the door.

The woman had fuzzy hair the color of rust and dark circles under her eyes. "Do you work for Mr. Bloodsaw?" Jeff wanted to know.

The woman looked down her crooked nose at Jeff and nodded. "My name is Wilma Fudgebottom. Let's just say I know this story. I'm here to make sure the make-up looks real." Her voice sounded like a door creaking open.

"I have to see Mr. Bloodsaw now," Jeff told Wilma. "Can't you do something?"

Wilma pointed a finger at him. Nina noticed the nail was jagged and yellow. "Wait your turn," Wilma told Jeff. "Like everyone else." Then she turned and walked away.

Nina shivered and pulled her sweater tight. "Why is it so cold in the hallway?"

Cassidy nodded. "It's bone-chillingly cold."

At those words, Nina and Cassidy

looked at each other with big eyes. There was only one thing that could cause this kind of shivers. Ghosts.

Nina tugged on Jeff's shirttail. After all, Jeff was their resident ghost expert. He had seen nearly every ghost movie ever made and had read even more ghost stories. "It's impossible for our ghosts to haunt the auditions," Nina said. "Isn't it?"

4
Ghostly Audition

Finally Jeff, Nina, Cassidy, and a few other third graders were called to the back of the stage by a skinny man named Sam. Sam was dressed in purple pants and a yellow T-shirt. "Steven Bloodsaw is a busy man," Sam said. "He has no time to waste."

"That's exactly what I've been saying all morning," Jeff snapped as he rushed past Sam. "Let's get this show on the road."

Jeff was more than ready. This was the moment he'd been waiting for all his life, but just before he marched to center stage for his audition, Nina gasped. "Look," she said, pointing to the rafters above the stage. "It's Ozzy and Becky."

Sure enough, the two ghosts from the basement hovered above them. Becky was smoothing hundred-year-old wrinkles from her shimmering skirt while Ozzy helped straighten the bows in her pigtails.

"What are they doing here?" Cassidy asked. "They can't get out of the basement!"

"Yes, they can," Jeff reminded her. "Ghosts can travel as long as they carry something from the time they lived."

Just then, Ozzy held up an object and

grinned. Cassidy knew exactly what it was. Ozzy had a piece of wood that had broken off her desk—the desk that once belonged to him. The ghosts had used it once before to escape the basement. They had made a mess of everything. Cassidy thought she had hidden the splinter in a safe place so the ghosts could never escape again. Ozzy had obviously found it, and he'd put his concentration powers on double duty in order to carry it.

"You can't be here," Cassidy whispered. "Give me back that wood."

Ozzy floated away. "I *have* to be here," he told them. "For Becky. This is her chance to be in that moving picture thing!"

"A ghost can't be in a movie," Jeff said with a sneer.

"Can so," Ozzy argued.

"Can not," Jeff told him.

"Do *not* tell us what we can and cannot do," Ozzy said.

Jeff was about to do just that when Sam called his name for the audition.

21

Jeff gave one last glare at the ghosts and made his way to the center of the stage.

Steven Bloodsaw, the director, sat in the front row. He looked up at Jeff through thick glasses framed in black. Wilma Fudgebottom stood in the shadows behind the director. "Please act as if you just saw a ghost," Mr. Bloodsaw said in a tired voice.

Jeff ignored Nina's giggle from behind the stage's thick red curtain. He had practiced making expressions a gazillion times in front of mirrors. He knew just what to do. Jeff put on his best scared face and reached his hands up to his cheeks. That's the exact moment that somebody tickled his ribs.

Ozzy!

Jeff did what anybody does when someone tickles them. He leaned over and grabbed his sides. When he did, he felt a kick in his rear end.

"What are you doing?" Sam cried as Jeff lurched forward. Of course, Sam couldn't see Ozzy.

Jeff didn't answer. He couldn't. He stumbled forward, but didn't get far because his shoelaces were mysteriously tied together. His arms flew out in crazy circles.

Becky nodded at her brother, smoothed her ghostly dress one last time, and then floated to stage front and curtsied.

"What is the meaning of this?" Mr. Bloodsaw snapped as he stood up from his director's chair.

Jeff tried to get his balance, but it was no use. He tripped and fell just as Ozzy tugged at his pant legs. That's when the worst thing that could happen to a kid happened.

Jeff's pants fell down. Luckily, Ozzy

chose that moment to wrap the stage curtain around Jeff.

Jeff wiggled and squirmed in the curtain, but he couldn't escape because Ozzy was sitting right on top of him. Nobody said a word. The gymnasium was silent except for muffled words from Jeff. Nina and Cassidy weren't sure, but they had a feeling it was a good thing that Mr. Bloodsaw couldn't understand what their best friend was saying.

Luckily, another noise drowned out Jeff. Wilma Fudgebottom was laughing. Not a little hide-behind-her-fingers kind of giggle, either. It was a hold-her-sides-so-they-don't-burst kind of laugh.

Wilma sat on the floor, tears streaming down the creases in her wrinkled face. "That's the funniest thing I've ever seen!" she said as she gasped for air. "You *have* to hire that one!"

5
Cut!

Two weeks had passed since the auditions, and the movie crew had begun shooting after school and on the weekends. But today was Jeff's first dress rehearsal.

"I'm going to be famous!" Jeff said, dancing around in the school basement.

Nina frowned at him. "Don't brag too much. You'll hurt Cassidy's feelings."

Nina glanced across the room at Cassidy. She was talking with the twins, Carla and Darla. For some reason, Mr. Bloodsaw, the director, had given Jeff the biggest part for an extra while Nina, Carla, Darla, and even Andrew had gotten smaller parts. Cassidy felt left out.

"Don't worry about Cassidy," Jeff said.

"She's doesn't even like movies. Just look at the basement. It's cool."

Nina looked around the classroom. When their class had first moved into the basement, Cassidy, Nina, and Jeff had convinced their teacher to decorate the room to look like it had over one hundred years ago. The classroom was filled with old-timey desks, pictures from long ago, and even a coal-burning stove that had been converted into a storage bin for art supplies. They had done such a good job that Mr. Bloodsaw had taken one look and decided to use it in his movie. He had even added a few touches of his own.

Fake cobwebs hung like curtains from the ceiling. Their teacher's desk had been turned into a mad scientist's laboratory table. A fake pipe organ sat in a corner. Nina knew that an actor dressed as a phantom would be pretending to play eerie music in one of the scenes. "It's interesting," Nina said slowly. She did not like scary things, and she definitely didn't like scary movies. "But I still don't see why Cassidy didn't get a part."

"Wow, there's the director now. Out of my way," Jeff said, totally ignoring Nina.

Nina sighed and stood in the hallway to watch the action. The lights in the classroom were turned down low and spiderwebs hung everywhere. Spiders gave her the creeps, and even though she knew they were movie props, she still felt uneasy. When a cold hand touched her on the shoulder, Nina screamed. "*AHHHH!!!*".

Everyone in the classroom looked at Nina as she turned around and realized it was just Cassidy. "Sorry," Nina whispered with a red face.

"Quiet on the set!" barked Sam, the director's assistant. Rehearsal continued inside the classroom.

Nina stood next to Cassidy and fumed. She shook her head, and her long black hair swirled around her face. "It's not fair," she whispered. "I don't even want to be a graveyard ghoul. My mom doesn't allow me to watch scary movies, and now I'm going to be in one. You should take my part."

"No way," Cassidy said. "You earned it."

"I'm going to have nightmares forever," Nina said.

Cassidy smiled. "Don't worry," she said.

"It'll be fun. I'll be watching from right here." The two girls peered through the classroom doorway. Wilma Fudgebottom, the strange lady with the crooked nose and wild hair, was watching closely as another costume artist painted Jeff's face to look like a ghoul. Jeff had white, white skin with green scars and deep-sunken eyes. Every once in a while, he shivered, although the bright movie lights were warm.

"Ooooh," said Nina. "Jeff looks like something bad dreams are made of."

"Look over there," Cassidy pointed. "A real nightmare is happening right in front of our eyes."

Becky floated over the middle of the set. Another ghost, Sadie, hovered nearby. Sadie had the reputation of being the saddest ghost ever. Her limp hair hung in strings over her gray face.

"Clear the set," Steven Bloodsaw ordered.

"Places, everyone!" Sam yelled through a megaphone.

Nina scrambled to her place, and Jeff made sure she and the other graveyard ghouls were behind him.

Costume artists, set designers, and Wilma Fudgebottom scurried out of the way as a woman aimed the huge movie camera at the set. Cassidy moved to the side as Wilma squeezed through the door, then stopped to watch over her shoulder.

Cassidy wiped away the goosebumps she got from the breeze made by so many people moving at once. Becky and Sadie floated above the fake pipe organ as the actors took their places. Cassidy didn't like the way Becky's eyes were narrowed into slits, but there was nothing Cassidy could do about it because just then Mr. Bloodsaw yelled, "ACTION!"

That was Jeff's cue to lead the gang of ghouls across the stage. Once they reached the far side, a gaggle of ghosts was supposed to come out and battle them. Cassidy knew the whole scene because Jeff had talked about nothing else for the last two weeks.

Jeff led Nina, Andrew, and the other ghouls across the room. They walked stiff-legged, staring straight ahead. Suddenly, five ghosts stepped out from behind a screen. They waved their arms like giant birds, letting the floppy sleeves of their costumes flap in the air. Everything went just as planned. At least, Cassidy thought so.

Wilma Fudgebottom, on the other hand, wasn't impressed. "No, no, no," she mumbled behind Cassidy. Her voice sounded like an old screen door, squeaking in the wind.

Cassidy looked over her shoulder. "What's wrong?" she asked. "The scene is perfect."

"Hmmph," Wilma grunted. "Perfect? What's perfect about that? Why aren't the ghosts flying? Why aren't they moving through the ghouls like the wind moves through trees?"

"Special effects like that would take more money and equipment than even a famous director like Steven Bloodsaw has," Cassidy said.

"But it doesn't look *real*," Wilma said. "What good is it if it isn't *real*?"

Cassidy wanted to tell her that *real* ghosts weren't all that much fun to have around, but she kept her mouth closed. She knew adults never believed kids when they talked about ghosts. "Maybe the ghosts would look more real if they had more of that white makeup on their faces," she said instead.

Wilma looked at the makeup cart that was sitting in the hallway. "Maybe," she said, as if she were thinking very hard about what Cassidy said. Then Wilma reached out and carefully selected a large bottle filled with white face powder.

Steven Bloodsaw was yelling directions again, and the actors were going back to their original places.

"Take two!" Sam yelled through his megaphone.

Cassidy settled back to watch the same scene. But the same scene didn't happen, because just then Becky dived down from her perch on the fake pipe organ. She swooped right in front of Jeff and the rest of the graveyard ghouls.

Jeff saw her and pushed her away, hoping that no one else noticed. Becky tumbled through the air like a wadded-up piece of paper. Just then, Ozzy flew into the room. He dived-bombed and hit Jeff full speed in the stomach! Jeff flew backward and collided with the fake pipe organ. The cardboard prop crumbled to pieces. That's when Wilma Fudgebottom dropped the huge bottle of white powder. It crashed to the floor and powder exploded everywhere. The

35

makeup floated over the movie set like a white cloud.

Nina couldn't help giggling a little, but she got very quiet when Mr. Bloodsaw screamed, "*Cut!*"

6
Carlos

"I cannot work under these conditions!" Mr. Bloodsaw screamed.

His assistant clapped his hands and said, "Let's break for lunch. We'll start back up again at one o'clock."

Most people moved upstairs toward the cafeteria. Even the ghosts disappeared into thin air. Jeff sat on the floor trying to pull the pipe off his head. Nina and Cassidy hurried toward Jeff, but Wilma Fudgebottom stepped in their way.

Her frizzy hair stuck straight out and the dark circles under her eyes made her look like she hadn't slept for a month. "Your friend is messing up everything," Wilma said. "Can't you do anything about it?"

Nina backed away from Wilma and shivered, but Cassidy spoke right up. "Jeff is trying his best," she said.

"Jeff?" Wilma said. "Who cares about him?" Wilma stalked away, but not before frowning in Jeff's direction.

Cassidy and Nina hurried over to Jeff. Cassidy pulled the paper pipe off his head. "Are you okay?" she asked.

Jeff pushed her away. "I don't have time for this. Can't you see I'm a busy man? And those ghosts are ruining everything. *Everything!*"

The three kids heard Sadie wail when Jeff stomped out of the room.

That's not the only crying they heard. Becky's sobs echoed around the room, too.

"Jeff doesn't like us," Sadie moaned.

"Jeff doesn't want to be our friend any more," Nina said sadly.

"I hope Ozzy does ruin the movie," Cassidy said. "It would serve Jeff right."

Just then the three kids heard a jangle. Or maybe it was a jingle. Olivia appeared with her newest unusual pet. "Thought I'd bring Carlos down to see all the action," Olivia said as she popped into the room. Olivia had been the school janitor for as long as anyone could remember. She liked taking care of animals — especially strange ones. The girls looked behind Olivia, but they didn't see any pets.

Olivia pointed to the strap on her bright red overalls. "Girls, meet Carlos!"

"Where is he?" Nina asked, squinting.

Cassidy didn't see anything, either. Then she noticed a little twitch and a quiver. Finally, she saw a tail nearly the color of Olivia's red overalls.

"Carlos is a chameleon," Olivia said. The chameleon suddenly jumped to the floor, and Nina squealed. Nina hopped onto a nearby chair as Carlos crawled onto a camera stand. Cassidy couldn't believe her eyes as the chameleon changed from red to yellow to gray. He took on the color of whatever he touched.

"Come here, Carlos," Olivia said.

The chameleon hopped off the stand and ran up Olivia's pant leg. It reappeared by Olivia's cheek.

"Poor Carlos," Olivia said. "He keeps changing from red to yellow to gray, trying to blend in. But the truth is, he'll never be my overalls or the floor or a camera stand. No matter how hard he tries, he'll always be just what he is. A chameleon. I just hope he doesn't forget how to be green! Of course, when he realizes he can't be anything except a chameleon, I'll be here. That's what friends are for. Right, girls?"

7
Forever Always

"Olivia talks to that chameleon as if it could understand every word she says," Nina said. "She acts like it's her best friend."

Cassidy shrugged. "If you ask me, a lizard would make a better friend than Jeff," she said. "He acts like he's too good for us just because he gets to be in a silly movie. I'm going to find him right now and give him a piece of my mind."

Cassidy didn't wait for Nina to answer. She marched up the steps in the direction of the cafeteria. The school was crowded with movie people. Nina followed her friend.

A group of actors dressed like zombies crowded around a coffee machine. Their gray skin looked so real that Nina had to

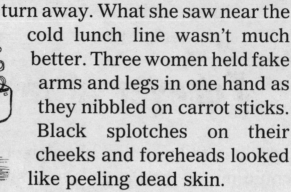

turn away. What she saw near the cold lunch line wasn't much better. Three women held fake arms and legs in one hand as they nibbled on carrot sticks. Black splotches on their cheeks and foreheads looked like peeling dead skin.

"Arrrgh," Nina said with a gulp. "Wilma Fudgebottom sure knows how to make things look real."

Cassidy giggled. "Have you looked at yourself in a mirror?" she asked. "Your skin is the color of mashed peas and your hair looks like it hasn't been brushed in three hundred years."

Nina's hand flew up to her hair to tug at a snarl. "Do I really look as scary as those other actors?" she asked.

"As soon as I put Jeff in his place, we'll find a mirror so you can see for yourself," Cassidy said.

The girls made their way through the crowded cafeteria. A goblin told them Jeff had been near the hot-dog stand. A zombie pointed toward the milk cooler. The costume designer thought she'd seen Jeff talking to Mr. Bloodsaw. Finally Cassidy asked Sam.

"Jeff?" the assistant said with a frown. "I know exactly where he'd better be. Rehearsing! I sent that troublesome ghoul back to the basement with a warning. If he doesn't stop causing trouble on the set, he's out of here. Now get lost. I don't have time for chitchat."

Cassidy and Nina hurried back down the steps. The girls had never gotten

used to the fact that their third-grade classroom was in the basement of Sleepy Hollow Elementary. They still didn't like the dingy hallway and deep shadows. But now it was even worse. The set designers had turned the entire basement into a living nightmare.

"Maybe we should wait until the rest of the crew comes back downstairs," Nina suggested halfway down the staircase.

Cassidy pulled Nina down the crumbling steps. "I'm not waiting to talk to Jeff. We've been friends too long to have it end like this."

The girls heard voices coming from a room at the far end of the hall. "It's Jeff," Nina whispered.

"Why isn't he practicing his lines in our classroom?" Cassidy asked.

Nina and Cassidy quietly opened the door a crack to peek inside the small storage room.

"You can't ruin my one and only chance. I've wanted to be involved in something like this my whole life," Jeff was saying to Ozzy. "Haven't you ever wanted something that badly?"

Ozzy pushed his nose right against Jeff's. "I know all about wanting things. And so does Becky. Now is *her* chance to have what she's always wanted."

"But she can't be in the movie. It's impossible," Jeff said.

Ozzy curled his hand into a ball and

slammed it into the wall. His fist sunk into the brick all the way up to his elbow. "You forget," Ozzy said, "that she's been waiting a lot longer than you have. It's time Becky got what she wanted."

"But what about me?" Jeff argued. "This is my chance to break into the movie business."

Nina heard a slurping sound when Ozzy pulled his arm out of the wall. "This isn't about you," Ozzy said. "It's about making my sister happy."

Cassidy and Nina jumped out of the way when Ozzy oozed through the door and floated down the hallway toward the classroom.

Cassidy was curious. "What is it that Becky wants?" she called after Ozzy.

He slowly turned and started to tell them, but he didn't get a chance because Andrew galloped down the steps. Ozzy disappeared like a giant soap bubble popped by a needle.

"Forget about him," Jeff said as he

pushed Nina and Cassidy aside. "In fact, forget about all of you! I'm too busy to worry about wishes and fairy tales. Come on, Andrew. We need to rehearse."

"Can you believe him?" Cassidy asked Nina after Jeff left with Andrew.

Nina sighed. "I believe Ozzy," she said. "It must be terrible wanting something for so long. I wonder what Becky wants."

"We have to find out," Cassidy said in a firm voice. "And that means finding Ozzy."

8
Ghost Tears

The girls glanced into the classroom. Andrew and Jeff had their backs to the door as they practiced their scene, walking across the room with stiff arms stretched straight out in front of them.

Nina stifled a giggle. "Look," she whispered, pointing at the organ inside the room.

Cassidy glanced at the cardboard organ. Huxley was busy sniffing the base of it. Ozzy's ghost dog never caused trouble. Well, almost never. Once in a while he did get a little carried away, especially when the ghost cat, Cocomo, was teasing him. Like now.

Cocomo swished her black tail in front of Huxley's nose. Her fur was tinged with a green glow, as if she had been sprinkled

51

with sparkling dust. Her tail left a trail of green glitter hanging in the air. Huxley reached for her tail just as the cat hopped away. Unfortunately, Huxley missed. He fell against the organ and it all tumbled down again.

"Oh, no," Jeff gasped. "Help me fix it."

"Why?" Andrew asked. "You knocked it over. Not me."

Jeff nudged the ghost dog out of the way before he pulled Andrew to the pile of cardboard. "But you're here. Steven Bloodsaw will blame both of us, and he'll kick us off the set. Hurry."

"Maybe we should help them," Nina whispered to Cassidy.

Cassidy pulled her friend back out to the shadows of the hall. "Serves Jeff right for forgetting who his real friends are," Cassidy said. "Besides, we need to find Ozzy."

A weak beam of sunlight struggled through the cracked window at the end of the hallway. Cassidy pushed cobwebs out of their way as they tiptoed toward the window. Except for the sounds of Jeff and Andrew struggling with the cardboard organ, the basement was shrouded in silence.

"It's quiet," Nina said. "Too quiet."

"Ozzy?" Cassidy whispered. "Where are you?"

Just then the girls heard a wailing sob. It came from behind the door to Olivia's workroom. Then they heard a long, sad moan: "Noooooooooooo."

Cassidy slowly pushed open the door. The room was full of shadows, but the glimmering shape of two ghosts could clearly be seen. Sadie hovered over Becky.

"Doooooon't cryyyyyyyyy," Sadie moaned.

Becky's hands covered her face. Tears flowed through her fingers and plopped on the floor. Her ghost tears grew bigger

and bigger the more she cried. A huge puddle had already formed on the floor.

Nina hated when anyone was sad. Even ghosts. "What's the matter?" she asked.

Becky sniffed and looked at Nina and Cassidy. Her eyes were rimmed in red. "Jeff said I couldn't be in the movie."

"Is that what you always wanted to be?" Cassidy asked. "An actress?"

Becky stifled a sob. "I want to dance. I want to be noticed. I want to be *somebody*. This is the only chance I've had. Ever!"

"We notice you," Nina said softly. "We know you're here."

Sadie tried to smile. "It isn't the same."

Cassidy looked at Nina. Nina looked at Cassidy. "Maybe you *can* be in the movie," Nina said.

Becky stopped sniffling. "Really?"

"How?" asked Sadie.

"You could be in the crowd scene with me," Nina said.

"But Jeff said I wouldn't show up,"

Becky said as new tears rolled down her face.

Cassidy pounded the palm of her hand with her fist. "There has to be a way," she said. "We'll figure out something."

Becky sniffed. She rubbed away the tears from her cheeks and started to twirl through the air. "I'm going to be in a movie!" she sang. Suddenly, she came to a dead stop. She turned from green to an alarming red. "But we have to find Ozzy!" she warned. "Before it's too late!"

"Why?" Cassidy asked, though she wasn't sure she wanted to know the answer.

"Because," Becky said with a whimper, "my brother said he was going to teach Jeff a lesson he would remember *forever*. And believe me, forever is a very long time!"

9
Surprise Ghost

"Hurry," Nina said. "We have to stop Ozzy!"

Cassidy rushed out of Olivia's office. Nina, Becky, and Sadie followed. They peered into every dark closet and corner in the basement, but they couldn't find Ozzy. Cassidy even lifted trash can lids to be sure he wasn't hiding inside. "Where can he be?" Cassidy asked.

Becky shrugged. "I looked for him for two days once when he was mad at me. I finally found him in the pencil sharpener."

"Isn't that dangerous?" Nina asked.

Sadie shook her head. "Not if you're a ghost."

"Oh," Nina said. "Maybe we'd better check the classroom."

"Andrew and Jeff are in there," Cassidy reminded her.

"We still have to look," Nina said. "Ozzy could be anywhere in the basement, and there's no telling what he has planned."

Cassidy, Nina, Becky, and Sadie rushed back toward the classroom. Just as they were ready to go in, they heard a loud commotion from the cabinet at the far end of the hall. "I bet that's Ozzy," Becky said.

"Let's get him," Cassidy said, running toward the old-fashioned cabinet. She flung it open and, sure enough, Ozzy was there, and he wasn't alone.

Wilma Fudgebottom and Ozzy tumbled out and circled the room like two wrestlers fighting for a championship belt.

"I can't believe it!" Cassidy yelped.

"It's the movie lady," Sadie moaned.

"Wilma Fudgebottom is a ghost! A *real* ghost!" Nina said with a gasp.

"That can't be," Cassidy said. "Everyone saw her."

59

Nina shook her head. "Think about it. We never saw her actually putting makeup on anyone. Steven Bloodsaw never talked to her. Sam didn't pay attention to her. Maybe that's because we were the only ones who could see her."

"Look out!" Becky yelled as green sparks flew from the end of Wilma's fingertips. Ozzy ducked and the sparks barely missed Cassidy.

Ozzy roared a battle cry that sent shivers up Nina's back. He charged at Wilma and sent her flying down the hallway. She snarled at Ozzy.

"Stop!" Cassidy yelled. "Why are you fighting?"

"I won't let him ruin my biography!" Wilma screeched.

"Biography?" Cassidy and Nina gasped at the same time.

Ozzy surged to ten feet tall. "If Becky can't be in the movie, then no one can!"

10
Makeup

"There's a way for me to be in the movie?" Becky asked after things had calmed down. She was so excited her glowing body trembled. Ozzy floated beside her and put his arm around his little sister's shoulders.

Wilma nodded. "I've been a ghost for a very long time. In fact, I even helped out a fellow named Shakespeare with some of his plays. Maybe you've heard of him."

Becky and Ozzy shook their heads and Wilma shrugged. "You will. I've learned a few tricks along the way. I've watched the best makeup artists there ever were. I can make you look dead if you're alive and alive if you're dead."

Cassidy was too curious to resist. "How?" she asked.

Wilma grinned and scratched her chin with a jagged fingernail. "I make a powder that covers ghosts so completely they show up on film."

Becky rushed at Wilma to give her a big hug. Unfortunately, Becky didn't stop soon enough, and she flew through the wall. She popped back out and tried again, more slowly this time. "This means so much to me," Becky said with tiny tears running down her face.

Wilma patted Becky's shoulder ever so gently. "There's one problem."

"What's that?" Nina asked.

"Your friend Jeff must agree to share the spotlight," Wilma said.

"Oh, no," Cassidy said. "He's too determined to be the star of this movie. Jeff will never do that."

Wilma's eyes blazed. "He must do it *my* way or I will not help you," she said.

Cassidy sighed. "Let's ask Jeff. It's worth a try."

Cassidy and Nina went into the classroom with Ozzy, Sadie, and Becky floating behind them. Jeff and Andrew were walking around the classroom like zombies. Cassidy went up to Jeff and whispered into his ear.

"No way!" Jeff snapped. "I'm NOT giving up my starring role!" Then Jeff stomped away from his friends and out of the room without even a second glance.

11
For Friendship

For the next week, Jeff refused to talk to the girls about the movie.

"They're filming that scene this morning," Nina said as she and Cassidy headed toward the school on Saturday. Rehearsals were over and the day had come to shoot Jeff and Nina's goulish scene. "If we don't think of a way to get Jeff's help, Wilma won't help Becky." Cassidy nodded grimly. "Ozzy will ruin it for everyone if his sister can't be in the movie."

"I can't believe Jeff chose fame over friendship," Nina said.

Cassidy stopped as if she had walked into a brick wall. "You know what? I can't either. Not the Jeff I know. I'm not giving up."

There was one thing Cassidy really hated

to do. Run. But Cassidy took off running so fast that even Nina had to pump her arms extra hard to catch up. When they reached Ghostville Elementary, they were both gasping for breath.

A group of kids in costume were clustered near the jungle gym. Jeff was in the middle. In the morning sunlight, his ghoulish makeup made him look like he had a bad bout of the flu. Cassidy didn't wait to catch her breath. She wiggled her way through the other actors, scattering ghouls and zombies without a second look, and stopped right in front of Jeff.

"You're going to listen, and you're going to listen good," Cassidy said. "Your future depends on it."

And then Cassidy did a very strange thing. She dropped her voice to a soft whisper so only Jeff and Nina could hear.

"Remember," Cassidy said, and she began talking about all the good times and the memories that Cassidy, Nina, and Jeff had had together. Jeff opened his mouth, ready to argue, but Cassidy's memories kept him from speaking. Finally, Cassidy stopped remembering.

"That is what makes a friendship," she said. "Are you willing to throw all those memories away?"

"Of course not," Jeff said.

"Then you have to do us a favor," Nina said softly. "A big favor."

The two girls explained how important it was for Becky to be in the movie.

"I can't give up my starring role," Jeff said. "This is a dream come true."

Cassidy put her hand on Jeff's shoulder. "We know that better than anyone," she said.

Jeff opened his mouth to argue, but Nina stopped him. "Think it through, Jeff. If you agree to Wilma's plan, then this could be the biggest scene in the movie."

Jeff looked at Nina. He looked at Cassidy. Then he shook his head. "Forget it," he said. "It would never work."

"Yes, it will," Cassidy told him. "But only if you agree to share the spotlight!"

12
Wilma's Story

Cassidy grabbed Jeff's arm. "We're late! There's no time to waste."

Sam clapped his hands three times. "Quiet on the set. Quiet on the set," he barked, even though nobody was paying any attention to him. Nina, Cassidy, and Jeff could hear him as they hurried down the hallway toward the classroom.

Cassidy pushed Jeff through the classroom door. "You're late! There's no time to waste."

Jeff hurried to his place in front of the other ghouls. Nina was right behind him.

Cassidy saw Wilma Fudgebottom in the shadows on the far side of the set where the ghosts were gathered. Her hair was frizzy, as if she'd been in a windstorm.

Wilma nodded at Cassidy. Cassidy nodded back, just as Steven Bloodsaw yelled, "ACTION!"

And that's exactly what happened. Action!

Jeff did exactly what they had rehearsed. When he was center stage, the ghosts slowly entered from the far side, ready to battle Jeff's graveyard ghouls.

Only Cassidy seemed to notice that there was one more ghost than before. It was Becky, and she was covered from head to toe in Wilma's special concoction of powder mixed with makeup goop.

The other ghosts slowly flapped their arms as if they were flying through the air. Not Becky. When she met Jeff at center stage, she actually floated into the air.

Steven Bloodsaw's eyes widened. Sam started fanning his face with the script. The rest of the actors stared as Becky towered above Jeff and the other ghouls. And then, right before their very eyes, Jeff rose into the air to battle Becky.

Ozzy used long, long arms stretched out to hold Jeff over the crowd of fake ghouls and ghosts. It was a scene straight out of a nightmare, except for one thing.

Becky and Jeff were grinning from ear to ear! Fortunately, nobody else saw it except for Nina and Cassidy.

After the scene, the director ran over to Jeff and shook his hand. "My boy, you're a genius. This scene needed special effects, but I couldn't afford them! How did you do it?"

Jeff held up the coil of rope Cassidy had given him to hold. "With this," he said, "and with a lot of help from my friends!"

Mr. Bloodsaw slapped Jeff on the shoulder. "You have a future in the movies," the director said. Then he handed Jeff a business card. "Save this. I have a feeling we'll be working together again someday!"

Becky, Ozzy, and Wilma Fudgebottom grinned at Jeff. But then the director looked over Jeff's head and straight at Becky.

"YOU!" the director said. "You were the best ghost out there. He reached out to shake Becky's hand, but Ozzy pulled her back. Together, Becky and her brother shrank away and were lost in the crowd of movie extras nearby.

That afternoon, the movie crew cleared out all the equipment and props from the classroom. They had scenes to shoot in the cemetery. Things were getting back to normal at Ghostville Elementary. Well, at least as normal as they could be in a haunted school.

"You were great," Nina told Jeff as they stood in the basement hallway.

No sooner were the words out of her mouth than green glitter filled the air. The glitter slowly became solid until it seemed real. Ozzy, Becky, and Wilma floated in the air before Nina and Jeff.

"Thank you," Becky told the kids. "You made my dream come true. You're *true* friends."

Ozzy blushed. "I owe you one," he said.

"No," Wilma Fudgebottom said. "I'm

the one who owes you all. Finally, my story will be told. Thanks to all of you!"

"What, exactly, *is* your story?" Cassidy asked.

"You'll have to wait," Wilma said with a sly grin, "and see the movie!"

About the Authors

Marcia Thornton Jones and Debbie Dadey got into the *spirit* of writing when they worked together at the same school in Lexington, Kentucky. Since then, Debbie has *haunted* several states. She currently *haunts* Ft. Collins, CO, with her three children, two dogs, one parakeet, and husband. Marcia remains in Lexington, KY, where she lives with her husband and two cats. Debbie and Marcia have fun with spooky stories. They have scared themselves silly with *The Adventures of the Bailey School Kids* and *The Bailey City Monsters* series.

Ready for more spooky fun?
Then take a sneak peek at the next

Ghostville Elementary®

#13 Guys and Ghouls

"What is your favorite monster movie?" Jeff asked Carla later that week. Jeff was surveying kids about their favorite scary movies for his project. He hoped to prove that scary movies were more popular than any other genre. Jeff, Carla, and Darla were sitting at a table in the back of their classroom.

Carla shook her head. "We don't have a favorite because..."

"... we never watch monster movies," Darla finished.

"Never?" Jeff asked. "That's ridiculous. What do you watch if you don't watch monster movies?"

Carla clapped her hands. "We just love..."

"...those movies about The Fearsome Four," Darla said.

"You mean you would rather watch cartoons about animal super-heroes?" Jeff asked.

As Jeff interviewed the twins, Ozzy popped into view. So did Sadie.

Sadie perched on a bookshelf so she was out of the way. Not Ozzy.

When the twins told Jeff how Chip the hamster saved the world, Ozzy grew hamster teeth, ears, and whiskers.

Cassidy and Nina couldn't help laughing. Even Sadie smiled at Ozzy's antics.

Ozzy wiggled his hamster nose as if he were sniffing at the twins' curly hair. Then he started nibbling on the girls' pigtails.

"Ouch," Carla squealed and glared at her sister. "Stop that!"

"I didn't do anything," Darla said.

"Yes, you did! You pulled my hair!" Carla said.

"I did not. You pulled my hair," Darla said back.

Jeff sighed as the twins marched to separate corners of the room in a huff. "They're the third and fourth girls to say they like The Fearsome Four," Jeff told Cassidy and Nina. "I can't believe girls like a cartoon better than a good old-fashioned monster movie."

"The Fearsome Four is funny," Nina said in a small voice.

"Not you, too!" Jeff gasped.

"Jeff's project is useless," Andrew said, plopping into a seat next to Cassidy. "Everyone knows that girls don't watch good movies. They're not smart enough."

Cassidy glared at Andrew. So did Sadie. Instead of crying, Sadie turned the color of dried-up spaghetti sauce. Ozzy, on the other hand, flexed a huge arm muscle as if he'd just won a wrestling match.

Cassidy knew girls were just as smart as boys, so she was determined to set Andrew straight. "You're the silly one who isn't smart enough," Cassidy told Andrew.

"Am not."

"Are too."

"Not."

"Too. You don't even have a project yet," Cassidy pointed out.

Andrew stuck his nose in Cassidy's face and grinned. "I didn't," he admitted, "but you just gave me the perfect idea."

Mr. Morton walked by and tapped their papers. "Back to work," he reminded them.

After Mr. Morton walked away, Andrew whispered to Cassidy. "You're going to be sorry you messed with me," Andrew said. "Very sorry!"

It's a boys-versus-girls battle

Big bully Andrew thinks that boys are better than girls— and Cassidy and Nina are determined to prove him wrong. But when classroom ghosts join the competition, they cause so much trouble that everyone realizes something's not right.

A ghost fight? Now *that's* scary! The competition is on—may the best ghoul win!